This book belongs to

SAM

WALT DISNEY®

FROM WHALES TO SNAILS

WALT DISNEY FUN-TO-LEARN LIBRARY

A BANTAM BOOK
TORONTO · NEW YORK · LONDON · SYDNEY · AUCKLAND

From Whales to Snails   A Bantam Book/January 1983   All rights reserved. Copyright © 1983 by Walt Disney Productions. This book may not be reproduced, in whole or in part, by mimeograph or any other means.

ISBN 0-553-05512-7

Published simultaneously in the United States and Canada. Bantam Books are published by Bantam Books, Inc. Its trademark, consisting of the words "Bantam Books" and the portrayal of a rooster, is Registered in U.S. Patent and Trademark Office and in other countries. Marca Registrada. Bantam Books, Inc., 666 Fifth Avenue, New York, New York 10103. Printed in the United States of America   0 9 8 7 6 5 4

Classic™ binding
R. R. Donnelley & Sons Company
patents U.S. and foreign pending

"Thar she blows!" yelled Dewey Duck. He was at the lookout post on Uncle Scrooge's yacht.

Everybody rushed to one side of the boat to see the spouting whales.

"What are those fish doing?" asked Louie.

Professor Ludwig Von Drake put on his spectacles and began. . . .

"Those are whales, not fish. Whales, unlike fish, must come up to the top of the ocean to breathe, just as land animals do. When whales spout, they are letting out the air they are holding in their lungs. But they take big breaths and can stay underwater for a long time.

"Whales are huge. The blue whale, biggest of all, is longer than nine elephants!"

"How can whales keep warm, deep under the cold water?" asked Daisy.

"They have a thick undercoat of fat, called blubber," said Ludwig.

"And what do whales eat?" asked Huey.

"Some whales strain 'sea soup' through the filters in their mouths," replied Ludwig. "Seawater is full of tiny animals and plants that these whales find good to eat. Some of the sea animals are so tiny you can see them only through a microscope. There are also whales that have teeth, and eat fish, squid, and other larger animals."

Whales are friendly animals. They usually live together in families called pods.

They "talk" to each other with clicks, moans, grunts, and songs.

"Quiet, please," said Donald. "I'm making a tape recording of one of their songs."

A baby whale is born tail first, instead of head first like many baby animals. It gets a chance to wiggle its body and get its muscles working before its head slips out of its mother's body.

Usually the other whales in the family are circling around to help the mother. One of them may quickly push the baby up to the surface to take its first breath of air.

The baby whale swims close to its mother's side. It plays with the other little whales and practices diving and leaping.

Dolphins are the smallest of the whales. They are clever and playful. All whales like each other's company. And they seem to like the company of people, too.

Dolphins have been captured and taught to do tricks.

And dolphins have even come to the rescue of swimmers in trouble by pushing them up to the surface of the water.

Orcas look like giant black-and-white rubber toys!
They, too, are clever at learning tricks.
They are sometimes called killer whales, because they
hunt other animals, such as seals.

Whales spend all of their lives in the sea. There are other animals that live in the water and on land, too.

Seals spend most of their lives in the water. But their white, furry babies are born on land. The mothers help them learn to swim.

Walrus, with their big moustaches and tusks, crowd together on rocks or ice floats.

At the South Pole, black and white penguins, which are birds, have wings so small they cannot fly at all! But they are wonderful swimmers. They walk upright on the ice and sometimes slide down snowbanks on their stomachs. When penguin chicks hatch, they sit on their parents' feet to keep warm.

There are more fish than any other animals in the sea.
Sharks are among the largest fish. They can be dangerous to
swimmers. Like other sharks, the great white shark has two
rows of very sharp teeth. Its body is long and streamlined, and
it moves fast.

Do you see that hammerhead shark? It has eyes and nostrils on "wings" sticking out from the sides of its head.

Unlike other fish, the shark's body is covered with tiny "teeth" instead of scales. The skin of a shark is as rough as sandpaper.

Some fish, like sharks, travel by themselves.
Others move in enormous schools, with millions of fish
swimming and twisting and turning in the water. There are so many
of them that they look like clouds in the sea!
Sardines, tuna, and herring swim in schools.

So do flying fish. They swim quite close to the top of the water. When they are being chased, they jump out of the water and into the air. They can "fly" for a short while to lose their enemies.

Some manta rays also leap out of the water. They come down again with a great *whomp!* that can be heard for miles.

Some of the rays have stings in their tails. But mostly they are gentle and harmless.

Fish travel all the time. Most of them live in rivers and lakes, or in the salty oceans.

"But here's a strange fish!" said the Professor. "The salmon is born in a little river, then travels out to sea, where it lives most of its life. It may grow very large and fat. And then one day, the salmon starts to make the journey all the way back to the stream where it was born! It may even have to leap up waterfalls to get there! But it is very tired and thin when it reaches the place where it was born. And there, after it lays its eggs on the sandy river bed, the salmon usually dies.

"The snakelike eel also makes a strange journey. It is born in a special part of the ocean called the Sargasso Sea. Here, eels come from far away to lay their eggs. When the eggs have hatched into little eels, or elvers, the elvers travel all the way back to the fresh waters where their parents grew up.

"More amazing still, elvers of 'American' parents go to America, and 'European' elvers go to Europe! And they never make mistakes and go to the wrong place!"

"I thought fish were supposed to live in water, not on land," said Donald.

"Most fish can breathe only in the water," said the Professor. "But mudskippers and lungfish and a few others can live in wet mud when the tide goes out."

Mudskippers poke their heads out of the mud to look around. Sometimes they leap right out of their holes and skitter along the beach. They splash themselves with water to keep their skins moist.

Sometimes mudskippers even climb trees!

Lungfish live among water plants or in small pools of water.

The lungfish can swim a long time underwater, but it must come up to the surface to take quick gulps of air.

If its pool dries up, the lungfish can "walk" on its fins until it reaches another watery spot.

"Let's stop off at Scrooge's Island and have a picnic," said Daisy. Everyone agreed it was a good idea.

As the Ducks were rowing toward the shore, they saw plants growing in the water. There was a buzz of insects. Suddenly an insect fell *plop!* into the water.

"It was shot by an archerfish," explained Von Drake. "The archerfish lies just beneath the surface of the water. When the archer sees a tasty insect, it shoots 'bullets' of water from a special tube in its mouth. Its aim is good, and the stunned insect falls into the water."

"A good snack for the archerfish," said Louie.

"Ah, food," said the Professor. "Fish have many ways of catching food. Mostly they swim around and eat whatever floats by. But the anglerfish lies on the bottom, with a 'fishing line' stretched out in front of its mouth. On the end of the line is a glob of flesh. A smaller fish comes to take a look at the 'bait' and—*swoosh!* It is sucked into the angler's mouth."

"I see a bird's nest under the water," said Dewey.

"No, it's a stickleback's nest," said Daisy.

Most fish lay their eggs in the water and then swim away. Sticklebacks are different.

The male builds a tunnel-like nest of grasses and roots. Then female sticklebacks, one at a time, come to lay eggs in the tunnel. When the nest is full, the father guards it fiercely. He fans the nest with his fins to keep water and air moving through it.

When the babies are hatched, the father stays near them until they can look after themselves.

Here are two more amazing little fish, the sea horse and the pipefish. They are close cousins. Both live in shallow water among sea grasses. And both are excellent fathers!

The females lay their eggs in the males' "pouches."

When the babies pop out, they stay near their father for a few days.

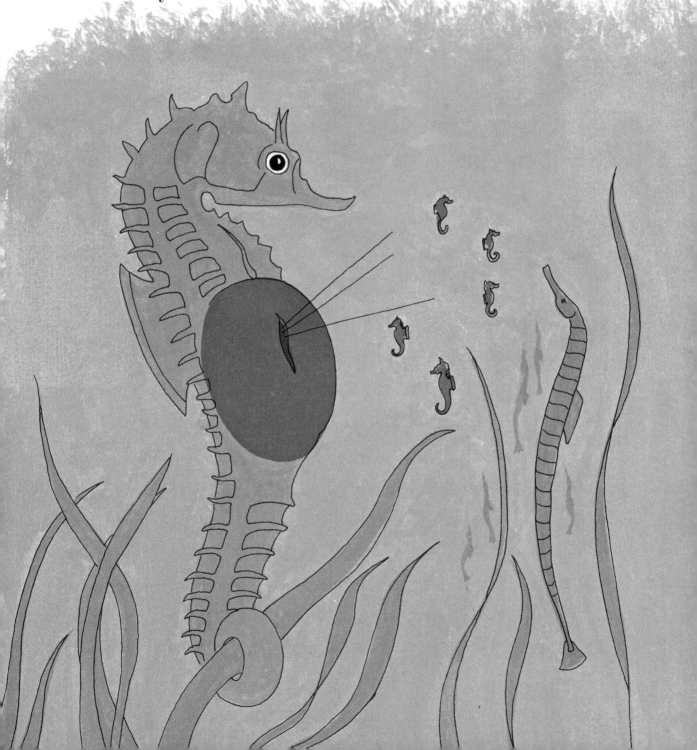

"Aha, here's a freshwater pond," said the Professor. "All kinds of creatures live their nursery days in ponds."

In ponds, frogs and toads grow from eggs to tadpoles to grown-up, land-living animals. Many fish live all their lives in ponds.

Tiny fish eggs may turn out to be big sunfish or carp.

"That carp looks just like my pet goldfish, only bigger," said Dewey.

"The goldfish is from the same family," said Von Drake. "Carp come in many shapes and sizes. People all over the world keep carp and goldfish in ponds."

"Here's a little snail," said Daisy. "It's carrying its 'house' on its back."

The snail can pull its soft body inside its shell.

When it wants to move, out comes its head and its foot. The foot is the lower part of the body. The snail makes a little path of slimy liquid as it moves along. This "snail trail" is like a smooth carpet for the snail to move on, even over sharp stones. When the snail has passed by, you might see the dried-up snail trail where it has been.

The snail's eyes are on two little stalks on its head. Inside its mouth is a sharp little saw that shreds its food.

Snails live in water or on land or both. You may find snail shells along the seashore.

Some snails have pretty colored shells. And some are so tiny you can hardly see them!

The snail's cousin, the slug, has no shell. It may live on land, or in the water.

"Well, you've arrived at last," said Uncle Scrooge. "I suppose you want to see my aquarium."

"Yes, please," said the Duck crew.

"I'd like to swim underwater like a fish," said Dewey. "But how do they breathe?"

"Fish get air through openings called gills," said the Professor. "The water in which they live is full of oxygen. A fish draws in water through its open mouth. It takes some of the oxygen from the water. Then the fish closes its mouth and the water escapes through its gills. Next question?"

"How can fish swim without arms and legs?" asked Huey.

spiny fin

back fin

gill

tail fin

belly fin

"They use all the muscles of their bodies to swing back and forth. They use their fins and tails as rudders. And their bodies have an air sac that helps them keep floating."

"Let's take a walk across the seashore," said Uncle Scrooge. "It's my favorite place on the island. Look at those green and white sand dollars all along the beach."

A fiddler crab waved its claw. Uncle Scrooge waved back.

Huey was really lucky. He found the biggest shell he'd ever seen.

"What's this?" asked Dewey.

"It's sometimes called a mermaid's purse," said the Professor. "But of course, there aren't any mermaids. It's the empty egg case of a shark or a ray."

    If you hold the pink inside of an empty conch shell to your ear, you may hear the sound of the sea waves.

    If you rub a speckled cowrie shell with your hand, it will become very shiny.

    All of these sea shells were once the homes of sea animals with soft bodies. Many of the animals that live in shells—clams, mussels, scallops, oysters—are good to eat, if they are found in clean water.

Sometimes an oyster makes a pearl inside its shell. A piece of rough sand gets inside the shell. The oyster doesn't like the way it feels, so it builds a smooth pearl around it.

But sometimes you just can't find that pearl, however hard you try!

"There are many more creatures in the sea that are not fish, though they sometimes have the word *fish* in their names," said the Professor.

The Portuguese man-of-war is a kind of jellyfish that looks like a tiny sailboat. The man-of-war travels fast and far across the ocean. Its "sail" catches the wind. Underneath the sail are long stinging tentacles. Some little fish travel along with the creature, feeding on scraps of food. They soon learn to keep away from those stings!

A starfish is sometimes called a sea star. It grips a mussel or clam with its arms and squeezes it open to get at the soft creature inside.

Lobsters may be small, or very large. They are covered with a light shell that moves about easily as the animals swim. The long feelers move slowly in the water as the lobster walks or swims on the sea bottom, looking for food. A lobster is usually grayish or green in color, but it becomes bright red when it is cooked.

Watch out for the big lobster's strong, pinching claws!

"Whack!" said Donald. "What's going on?"

"That dark cloud was made up of octopus ink," explained the Professor when Donald described his adventure. "Of course, it isn't like the ink that you write with. It is a dark-colored liquid. The octopus may look fierce, but it is a shy creature. When it is scared, it makes a cloud of ink so you can't see it."

The octopus has eight long arms, called tentacles. It uses the suckers on its tentacles to hang onto rocks or onto its food.

The octopus mother lays her eggs in a hiding place. She stays nearby to see that they are safe.

The squid, like the octopus, may be tiny—or it may have tentacles as long as a bus! Both animals are clever, with large eyes, parrotlike beaks, and big brains.

"Now we are going to explore deep into the ocean," said Von Drake.

"As you can see, the ocean has mountains and valleys just like those up above, where we live. The sunlight doesn't reach down here. Yet there are plenty of fish. Some of them glow with light, like fireflies. Some have long, sharp fangs and strange shapes."

"Isn't that a treasure chest?" asked Dewey.

"And Uncle Donald found the treasure!" said Huey and Louie, laughing, as Donald ran from an angry octopus.

The Duck crew put on its flippers and masks and set out to explore the coral reef in search of more adventures.

Coral reefs are the gardens of the sea. The waters around them are warm and clear.

Among the stony corals live brightly colored fish, some spotted, some striped, some with fins like trailing wisps of cloud.

You may see sea anemones, little animals that look like flowers, and slow-moving sea cucumbers. Many black sea-urchins cluster together, their spines moving slowly as you pass by.

"Well," said Daisy when they came up for a rest. "We may not have found gold or precious stones, but this beautiful coral reef is the real treasure of the sea!"